W9-DFG-758

BASEBALL CARD CRAZY

Trish Kennedy and Timothy Schodorf

BASEBALL CARD CRAZY

CHARLES SCRIBNER'S SONS • NEW YORK
Maxwell Macmillan Canada • Toronto
Maxwell Macmillan International
New York • Oxford • Singapore • Sydney

Charles Scribner's Sons Books for Young Readers
Macmillan Publishing Company
866 Third Avenue, New York, NY 10022

Maxwell Macmillan Canada, Inc.
1200 Eglinton Avenue East, Suite 200
Don Mills, Ontario M3C 3N1

Macmillan Publishing Company is part of
the Maxwell Communication Group of Companies.
10 9 8 7 6 5 4 3 2
Printed in the United States of America

Library of Congress Cataloging-in-Publication Data
Kennedy, Trish.
Baseball card crazy / Trish Kennedy and Timothy Schodorf.
—1st ed. p. cm.
Summary: While staying with his grandparents on their farm, fifth grader Oliver O'Malley searches diligently for the long-lost baseball card collection his father amassed as a boy.
ISBN 0-684-19536-4
[1. Baseball cards—Fiction. 2. Grandfathers—Fiction.
3. Grandmothers—Fiction.] I. Schodorf, Timothy. II. Title.
PZ7.K3864Bas 1993 [Fic]—dc20 92-14597

BASEBALL CARD CRAZY

Has this ever happened to you?

You show your collection of baseball cards to a grown-up guy, and he proceeds to tell you about the great baseball cards that *he* had when *he* was a kid. He names about four or five different fantastic cards, which are extremely rare today, and valuable, and for which you would give just about anything. And then he says that if he had those cards today, they'd be worth a fortune, and he'd be a millionaire.

Has that ever happened to you? It happens to me all the time. Constantly. My own father is the worst. To hear him tell it, he had the baseball cards for every great player from his era. (His era was the late fifties and early sixties.) He used to buy Super Chew bubble gum, which he says cost five cents back then. I can't believe it; for a nickel, you could get ten baseball cards, plus a big, juicy wad of bubble gum. That's how you did it back in the old days. The main thing was the bubble gum. You bought the gum, and you'd get the cards as a bonus. Anyway, Dad bought mass quantities of those Super Chew packs and saved all the cards. He traded some of them and kept others. Apparently, he was a real wheeler-dealer, because he managed to trade his way to an incredible collection, a collection that would be very valuable today—that is, if he still had it. But that's the problem: He *doesn't* have it. Dad didn't save any of those great cards. And that just about breaks my heart, because I, Oliver O'Malley, am what you would call a serious baseball card collector. I have what I'm sure is *the* most serious baseball card collection in the fifth grade at Millard Fillmore Elementary School. Maybe it's even the best collection in the whole school.

I have a lot of friends who also collect baseball cards. But they're not serious about it, not really. Not like me. You see, I study all the statistics. I know which players are at the top of their game and which are on their way downhill. I know which rookies are showing potential and how far they'll probably go in the major leagues. Please understand, I'm not bragging. I just know these things, because collecting baseball cards is more than just a hobby with me; it's my main interest in life, and I spend a lot of time on it. In fact, you can name just about any player, and I can tell you what team he plays for, how long he's been playing, his height, weight, age, and batting average. Maybe I can even tell you what he eats for breakfast.

My mother says my huge interest in collecting baseball cards is more than a hobby; it's what she calls an obsession. In fact, she told me, "Oliver, what you are is just plain baseball card *crazy*!" She keeps saying that if I devoted as much time to my schoolwork as I do to my card collection, I'd be a genius. And Mom thinks we could definitely use a genius in the family. She may have a point, but I like to think that all the studying of statistics and facts that I do is good training for my future career. What my future career will be, I'm not sure of yet. But I just know that card collecting has got to be good training for it. However, I don't think you can actually get paid to collect baseball cards.

I have a little sister, who's seven, named Samantha. I usually call her Sam. She doesn't like the name Sam too much. She thinks it sounds like a boy's name, and she thinks of herself as a very girlie kind of girl. She has long, golden hair that Mom brushes a hundred times every night so it will be shiny. I guess Sam wants to glow in the dark or something. She and Mom spend a lot of time on that hair, curling it and braiding it and attaching little ornaments to it. Actually, I think they spend about as much time on Sam's hair as I do on my baseball card collection.

Sam wears dresses with a lot of ruffles and lace and stuff, and she wears cute little shoes with bows on them. And she has to have everything pink—her toothbrush, her book bag, her lunch box. So I'm sure you're not surprised when I tell you that my little sister thinks that anything having to do with baseball cards is pretty boring and silly. She thinks that any cards you can't play Go Fish with are a complete waste of time. *Her* main interest in life is her collection of Cabbage-Face dolls. She has four of them. I know that's not their correct name, but that's what I call them, because each one is uglier than the last. They've got these little pushed-in faces that look like someone squished them with a steamroller. Samantha thinks they're cute. Sometimes Mom has to put an extra dinner plate on the table for a Cabbage-Face, and after it's finished eating, Samantha tries to get it to burp, for pete's sake. She really thinks the thing is actually going to burp or something. I sincerely hope she gets over this condition someday.

Anyway, back to my card collection. I've been working on it for several years now, ever since the first grade. The older I've gotten, the more serious I've become about it. I subscribe to *Baseball Card Weekly*, which lists the current value of every card. It has articles about which players' cards are increasing in importance. The articles also tell about printing errors and other things that make a card's value go up or down. And they have a lot of other interesting information. Every few weeks, I total up the values of all my cards, just so I can keep tabs on what my collection is worth. My parents just kind of laugh when I tell them my collection is probably worth over a thousand dollars. I don't think they believe it. They say things like, "Well, that's on *paper*, Oliver. Not in actual dollars." Or, "Maybe someday, Oliver, but it's not worth that much *now*."

Even though they don't actually believe my collection

is valuable, at least not at the present time, my mother and father do think my hobby of collecting cards is a pretty good idea. Dad keeps saying that the way I study card values and statistics, I'll be a whiz if I ever decide to play the stock market. I don't know about that; I don't really understand too much about the stock market. But I know they think collecting baseball cards is a much more worthwhile pastime than, say, watching wrestling on television or dropping water balloons out of second-story windows.

I know I talk a lot about the value of my cards, but that's not the main reason I got into collecting. I really love baseball. I love everything about it. I've played in Little League since the first year I was big enough. I watch a lot of baseball on television. I like to sit in my room sometimes and just look through my card collection and fantasize about what it would be like to be a professional baseball player. I imagine swinging a bat at home plate at Wrigley Field on a warm June day. I think how it would feel to have thousands of people in the stands, cheering for me: "O-Mal-LEE! O-Mal-LEE! Hit one outta here!"

I race Dad to the sports section of the paper every morning. If I get up early enough and get to the paper before he does, I get to read the sports section, and he's stuck with the business section. Fortunately, he finds the business section pretty fascinating. I can't see it, myself, but he likes it. So he doesn't mind too much when I get to the sports first. Unless, of course, there was a big title fight or a World Series game or something the night before. I go over all the scores of the previous day's games and read the latest news about who's being traded or who's about to break a major league record.

I've even been to the National Baseball Hall of Fame in Cooperstown, New York. It was during my family's summer vacation two years ago. We drove all the way there from Ohio. The trip took a long time, because the rest of my family wanted to see some other things along the way, like Hershey, Pennsylvania, where they make the chocolate and Niagara Falls. Sam whined the whole way to the Hall of Fame because she'd left one of her precious Cabbage-Faces in the motel room we stayed in at Niagara Falls. I told her it must have overslept and missed the wake-up call. That only made her whine louder. Mom assured her that she would call the motel and that the manager would keep the Cabbage-Face for her, and we would pick it up on our way back to Ohio. But Sam kept whining anyway; she was worried about her little baby. I don't know what she thought was going to happen to it, maybe that someone was going to kidnap it and hold it for ransom or something. Aside from the Cabbage-Face problem, however, the trip was a lot of fun. The Hall of Fame is incredible; they have Babe Ruth's original bat and the glove used by Cy Young. They even have Maury Wills's spikes. It's a very impressive place.

One of my favorite things of all is going to baseball card shows. You can really have fun at a card show. They usually have them at shopping malls or someplace like that. There are a lot of different booths and displays, and people come from all over the country to trade baseball cards. I check out all the booths to see which cards I'd be interested in adding to my collection. Usually I take along a stack of my own cards, which are good ones, but ones I wouldn't mind trading if the right deal came along. Then I go around and try to make trades with different dealers. I've made some awesome trades at baseball card shows. One time I picked up a mint-condition 1978 Reggie Jackson by trading a Ricky Henderson from 1985. I didn't mind letting go of my Ricky Henderson because I happened to have a duplicate. Another time I traded for a 1982 Cal Ripken, Jr., and two weeks later the value of that card went up ten dollars, according to *Baseball Card Weekly*. Sometimes I've taken money I've saved up from my allowance to card shows, so I could buy special collector cards. But I think it's really more fun to trade cards than buy them.

Another thing I like about baseball card shows is that you get to see some really spectacular cards, up close and in person. The dealers keep them locked up in glass cases to protect them. I can't afford to buy any really valuable cards, not yet, at least. But it sure is exciting to see, inches away from me, an original Roger Maris from 1962, or a Ted Williams, in perfect condition, from 1958.

I really have to admire the grown-up guys who, when they were kids, put the baseball cards they had collected away in a safe place, so they'd be in good condition today and worth a lot of money. I know there must have been at least a few guys who did that because of all the people who have those booths with all the great cards at the shows. Some guys in the world managed to hang on to their cards, but certainly not any of the guys I ever meet. Everyone I meet tells me that same old sad story about how they used to have all those rare and valuable cards, and how their moms threw them away, and how they'd be rich today if only she had saved them. I have to admit, the moms usually are the ones who take the rap for losing the cards.

One Saturday last May, a few weeks before school let out for the summer, Dad and I were driving to a baseball card show at a shopping mall in a nearby town. Dad had already heard plenty of times from me about how I wished he had saved his baseball cards and not let them get lost forever. However, it had been on my mind a lot lately, and I brought up the subject again, for about the five-hundredth time.

"You know, Dad, if *I* had been a kid during the fifties and sixties," I said, giving him a meaningful glance, since he *had* been a kid during the fifties and sixties. "If *I* had been a kid back then, I would have saved every baseball card I could have gotten my hands on. I would have made sure I collected Stan Musial's rookie card. I would have somehow managed to get a Yogi Berra. And I know for sure I would have traded something to get a Mickey Mantle, and I would have put it away in a safe place, so it would be in perfect condition today. Yeah, that's what *I* would have done, all right."

Dad just kind of chuckled to himself and kept driving. He must have decided it was time to eat, though, because at that moment, he turned into the parking lot of McDonald's.

"I hear what you're saying, Oliver," Dad said as he squeezed the car into a little parking place between two vans. "You just *think* you would have known enough to save your baseball cards. Hindsight's twenty-twenty, you know."

What does *that* mean? I thought to myself. I had to think about that for a minute. Dad is always sprinkling his conversation with little sayings that are supposed to relate to what you're talking about, but you have to stop and figure out why. My grandad, who's my father's dad, does that a lot, too. I guess it runs in the family.

"Hope you're hungry, Ollie," said Dad as we walked into McDonald's. "I'm so hungry I could eat the Empire State Building and have the World Trade Center for dessert. How about you?"

I wasn't too hungry, at least not hungry enough to eat a building, not even one of the golden arches from the building we were in. You have to hand it to Dad, though. He really has a picturesque way of expressing himself. I wasn't really in the mood to stop and eat, because I was in a hurry to get to the card show. But I could see that Dad was having one of his famous Big Mac attacks, and the best thing to do when that happens is to humor him. He can get a little cranky when he's hungry; fortunately, a hamburger with mustard and pickle can put him back into a good mood.

I myself don't have the best feelings about that particular McDonald's, because of an incident that happened there to my mother and me about a year ago. Before we had our lunch, I removed my dental retainer. It's the kind you have to take out of your mouth in order to chew. I set the retainer down on my tray, but my mother decided it didn't look too pleasant while she was eating, so she covered it up with a napkin. This particular type of retainer comes in a lot of different colors and styles. The dentist lets you choose which model you want. They had the Tiger model, which was yellow and black striped, the Leopard, with spots, the Zebra, black and white swirls, and so forth. I'd picked the Alligator retainer, which was kind of a strange mixture of green and brown blobs, and—Mom was right—not too appetizing. Sitting on the tray like that, it kind of looked like a big toad or something. You kept expecting it to hop away.

Anyway, since Mom had covered the retainer with a napkin, when it came time to leave, we forgot about it. I emptied it into the garbage container along with the rest of the trash on my tray. We were halfway home when I suddenly realized my retainer wasn't in my mouth. We had to rush back to McDonald's and explain what had happened. One of the employees, who was trying real hard, I could tell, not to laugh, showed us out to the back where the trash had already been emptied into a big Dumpster. Boy, I'll say one thing: They are certainly fast with the trash, as well as the food, at good old McDonald's. Mom looked at the bulging Dumpster and then looked at me, and she reminded me that the retainer had cost four hundred and fifty dollars. So we spent the next hour and a half searching through a ton of McDonald's trash for my retainer. We finally found it, but that was an experience I'd really like to forget.

Dad and I got our burgers and fries and sat down to eat. Between bites, we continued our conversation about baseball cards and Dad's lack of foresight in not saving his.

"You know, Oliver," he said, "if you had been a kid when I was, I doubt very much whether you would have been brilliant enough to hang on to your old baseball cards, either."

I wasn't so sure about that. Maybe he was right. Maybe.

He went on, "Every guy I know regrets not saving his baseball cards from when he was a kid. But no one realized then that card collecting was going to be such a big thing years later. And another thing, when some-one like Mickey Mantle is just starting out in his career, no one knows if he's going to hit the big time or not. Nobody knows that until years later, after the guy has already gotten famous. And if you're going to invest in a valuable collector card, you have to buy it long before anyone knows that the guy is going to be great and that his card is going to be worth a lot of money."

Well, that was true. Dad did have a point there.

"Back in my day," said Dad, "kids saved their base-ball cards for a while, but then they'd get a little older, and they'd lose interest in collecting. Saving cards was kind of a little kid thing to do, back then. So when kids got tired of their cards, they just lumped them in with a lot of other old junk they didn't play with anymore. My own collection took up a lot of space, and I didn't have a whole lot of space to begin with."

Now Dad's voice was changing from its lecturing mode to a more sentimental, nostalgic tone. It always got that way whenever he started talking about the good old days when he was a boy and lived on his family's farm.

"You know what we used to do with our baseball cards?" he said. "We used to attach them to the spokes of our bike wheels with clothespins. They made a loud, clackety sound that sounded just like a motorbike."

I groaned. I could just picture a 1958 Hank Aaron, stuck between the spokes of some kid's bicycle. Didn't those fifties kids have any respect?

"Of course, I didn't do that to my *best* cards," said Dad quickly, as if he knew what I was thinking. "Gosh, when I think about some of the cards I had—awesome cards. You know, I had some of the best cards that were made back then."

Yeah, I knew. Now he was getting to the part that always broke my heart.

"I saved every single card I had, for a while. But they started taking up too much room. So then I threw away a lot of less important cards and just kept the really good ones. I had Willie Mays's rookie card, can you imagine that? Boy, if only I could get my hands on that card today. What a collector's item! And I had a Joe DiMaggio. I loved that card. It had a wonderful photo of him at home plate in Yankee Stadium. I remember, I used to have a Flintstones book bag. I'd put my cards in that and take them to school. I had to keep them in the book bag, because you could get into serious trouble for having baseball cards in the classroom."

Yeah, Dad, I thought to myself. You could probably get the electric chair for that in this state.

"At recess," Dad went on, "we'd all take our cards out to the playground so we could compare them and make trades. I'll have to say, I made some of the best trades around. I figured out, for instance, that Lou Brock was going to be a star, long before any one else did. I saved the first card I ever had of Bill Mazeroski, before anyone knew who he was, and long before he hit a home run to win the World Series for the Pirates in 1960. I put together a fantastic collection; it had some of the best cards ever printed—"

"Dad," I interrupted, "what *happened* to those cards? I mean, the rare ones. What happened to the really good cards you had, the valuable ones, the ones you saved?"

"I don't remember, exactly," said Dad thoughtfully.

I knew he'd say that. He *always* said that. I don't know why I kept asking him about those cards. I guess I thought that one day he'd suddenly remember, that he'd have a brainstorm. I kept hoping that one day the location of his long-lost baseball cards would suddenly dawn on him.

"I sure did have some great cards, though," said Dad, shaking his head regretfully. "I had a Yogi Berra that everyone was always trying to get me to trade. And there was another one that everyone I knew wanted—a 1958 Whitey Ford."

"Whitey Ford!" I hid my face in my hands and groaned again in frustration. "Dad! Can't you think back—think really hard—and just *guess* what might have happened to your baseball cards?"

"Well," he said, "if I had to guess, I'd guess that the same thing happened to my collection that happened to everyone else's. Somewhere along the way, the cards just disappeared, faded out of sight. Either our parents got rid of them, or they were packed away in a box that was lost somewhere, or something like that. Anything could have happened. It's hard to tell."

I pictured landfills all over the United States with boxes and boxes of old baseball cards, cards that I would do almost anything to get my hands on. I pictured deserted attics, full of valuable collector cards stashed away in boxes, buried under piles of rubble, never to be seen again.

"Dad," I moaned, "don't you realize how frustrating this is? You *must* remember what you did with your cards. Just one teeny-weeny little Ted Williams. Please!"

"Sorry, Ollie," Dad said cheerfully. Obviously, *he* wasn't going to lose any sleep over lost baseball cards. "Come on, let's get going."

We took our trays to the trash container. I gave my tray one last going-over just to be safe, even though I knew my retainer was tucked away in my side pocket.

"I just didn't care that much about them at the time," said Dad as we got into the car to leave. "I stopped being interested in baseball cards after I got to high school. I started being more interested in other things."

He means girls, I thought to myself.

Dad continued. "Those cards might have been put away in the attic or something, but I really feel that Gram probably threw them out sometime when she was spring cleaning. I know one thing: I didn't take them with me when I grew up and left home and got married."

Why *not*? I thought to myself. Why couldn't you have taken those cards with you and given them to your little kid, so he could have had the best baseball card collection in town, maybe the best collection in the whole state of Ohio? I couldn't stop thinking about it.

"Well, it's too late now," said Dad. "It's just water under the bridge. And there's no use crying over spilt milk, is there?"

Those little sayings of his are supposed to make you feel better, I guess, but in this case, it didn't make me feel better at all. Dad and I drove the rest of the way to the mall and found the baseball card show. Dad went off to do some shopping, and I started to look around at what was there. There were a lot of booths set up; it was a pretty big show. There were a lot of rare cards on display. I looked through one of the glass cases at a 1949 Duke Snider, which sold for nine hundred and seventy-five dollars. I couldn't help wondering if maybe my Dad had had that very card. If he had, where was it today? At the bottom of a cardboard box in a dusty basement, I thought sadly.

But wait a minute. Suddenly, I started thinking. Maybe that collection of cards Dad had *was* still around someplace. Maybe it hadn't ended up at the bottom of the city dump after all. Dad had lived all his life—well, till he was nineteen or twenty, anyway—in the same house, and his parents still lived there. What if, by some miracle, those cards *hadn't* gotten thrown out? What if they were still at my grandparents' house somewhere? Could they actually still exist?

I picked up two or three fairly good cards at the show that day by trading some that I had brought with me. But my heart wasn't really in it. As I wandered from booth to booth, my mind wasn't really on what I was seeing. I was too busy thinking about the possibility of finding Dad's baseball cards.

Dad and I met up at the mall entrance. While I had been cruising the show, he had been looking at weed killers and garden tools. I told him I'd been thinking about his card collection, and how I thought we should make an effort to try and find it.

"Now that would be a big waste of time," he assured me. "They'll never turn up, Oliver. Don't torture yourself thinking about it. They're gone, son."

"But, Dad!" I didn't want to nag him. He hates nagging. "Just let me do one thing. Please! One thing!"

"What's that?" he asked.

"The next time you talk to Gram and Grandad on

the phone," I said, "let me talk to them for a minute. Just for a minute, so I can ask them if they remember anything at all about those cards. You never know. Maybe they'll remember what happened to them."

My grandparents live on a farm in southern Ohio, about a hundred and fifty miles from where we live. It's long distance to talk to them, so it's not like I can just pick up the phone and say hello anytime I want to.

Dad shook his head like he thought the whole idea was pretty hopeless. But he didn't say no. He said, "Well . . . Okay, Oliver. Next time I talk to Gram and Grandad, you can ask them. But don't get your hopes up, okay? That was a long time ago."

Well, maybe Dad thought there was no hope, but I was pretty excited. Somehow, I just knew those baseball cards *couldn't* be lost forever. And maybe, if I thought really hard and was very determined, I just might be able to figure out where they had gone.

CHAPTER 2

As it turned out, I got my chance to ask Gram about Dad's baseball cards a lot sooner than I had thought.

About a week after Dad and I went to the baseball card show, he found out that he had to make a business trip to New York City. He had to be gone for three weeks, so he was going to take Mom with him. They decided that while they were there on business, they would have some fun, too. You know, grown-up kind of fun—shopping, going to symphonies and plays, and other boring kinds of stuff.

Anyway, they decided that Samantha and I would stay with Gram and Grandad at their farm for the three weeks they would be gone, which I thought was a terrific idea. Even if I hadn't been eager to get to their house to look for Dad's baseball cards, I would have still thought it was a terrific idea to visit Gram and Grandad. So, Dad was happy, Mom was happy, and I was happy. The only one who wasn't happy was Sam, who started in whining right away. The major reason she wasn't happy about going to our grandparents'—aside from the fact that she is automatically negative about *everything*—was that our visit was for the first three weeks of summer vacation. She and her best friend, Tiffany Bonaventure, had cooked up a bunch of different activities they wanted to do, each one more stupid than the last. They were going to stage some sort of Cabbage-Face beauty contest, complete with a talent competition. Then they had plans after that for a neighborhood jump-roping tournament and had already sold a bunch of tickets for it. Girls can think of some of the dumbest ways to have fun.

Dad telephoned Gram and Grandad to work out the details of our visit. I stood next to him as he spoke to Gram, frantically gesturing so he'd remember that I was supposed to have a chance to talk for a minute. When Dad finished making the arrangements with Gram, he handed the phone to me and said I could speak for two minutes, and two minutes only.

"Let's see," Gram said slowly, when I asked her if she had any idea what had happened to Dad's baseball card collection. "Baseball cards. Baseball cards . . . Yes, I remember lots of baseball cards."

Come on, Gram, I thought to myself. I've only got two minutes, for pete's sake.

"Let's see," she went on. "Your father used to play

with a whole group of boys who collected cards. He used to take them to school all the time in his—"

"I know," I said impatiently. "In his Flintstones book bag! But where are those cards *now*, Gram? Did you throw them away, or do you think you might still have them?"

"No," she said. "I don't believe I would have thrown them away. But I really don't have the foggiest idea what we *did* do with them. Are you sure your father doesn't have them somewhere?"

"Yes, I'm sure," I said, and sighed. This conversation was going nowhere. But at least Gram didn't remember throwing the cards away. That was one good thing. That meant that maybe the cards were still there, at their house. It was a fact that they lived in the same farmhouse they had always lived in, ever since before my dad was born. They had never moved, and that's when people usually throw things away. At least, that's when *my* mother throws things away. A lot of my favorite things have disappeared forever during a move to a new house. Parents think you aren't going to notice when they throw away a complete set of Ninja Turtles, or the Batmobile it took you two whole days to put together. Has this ever happened to you? One day you suddenly decide you want to play with your G.I. Joe Skystriker, and you look all over the place for it—and it's gone! Your mother says, "Oh, yes, we threw that out when we moved. Don't you remember?" At least I know for sure that none of my baseball cards has ever been tossed in the garbage. Even my mother knows better than to throw away a baseball card. But I'll bet you anything that's how a lot of kids' baseball card collections bit the dust.

Anyway, I decided right then that there was every chance in the world that those cards might just be lying around in Gram's attic, waiting for me to discover them.

I was even more encouraged a few nights later, when I was watching the news on television. Well, actually, Dad was watching the news. I was kind of halfway listening while I played Monopoly with Samantha and her favorite Cabbage-Face at the kitchen table. I was beating the socks off both of them. It was really no contest; Monopoly is my second most serious hobby, after baseball cards, and I'm pretty good at it, if I do say so myself.

Anyway, there was this story on the news about a kid in Massachusetts or Maine or someplace who had found a Honus Wagner card from 1910, buried in a box in his backyard, for pete's sake. The card, not even in great condition, turned out to be worth over two hundred thousand dollars. One little card! Wow, I was impressed. This was very inspiring, but at the same time, it made me even more frustrated. That kid could have been me. I started thinking so hard about finding lost baseball cards that Sam landed on Park Place and bought it without me even noticing. When I finally turned my attention back to the game, the Cabbage-Face had suddenly moved into first place, and I was in jail.

♦

Finally, the day came for us to drive to Gram and Grandad's for our three-week visit. We all piled into the car. Samantha took up three-fourths of the backseat with her dolls and all the junk that went with them—the clothes for the dolls, the houses and cars of the dolls, the pets of the dolls. Besides her regular group of Cabbage-Faces, Sam had brought along these scented dolls she has that are supposed to smell like perfume, but instead have the odor of spoiled fruit. I had to spend most of the trip with my head hanging out the car window, trying not to gag. Sam started playing with the automatic window controls and came close to strangling me. As usual, when I howled in protest, Mom and Dad said, "Don't be mean to Samantha, Oliver. She's younger than you are." I guess being younger entitles you to get away with almost anything, even attempted murder.

Gram and Grandad live in a great place. Their farm is on a lake, and it's a great lake, although I like it better for fishing than for swimming. The water is kind of brown and murky, and you have to wonder what's in there. They have some neighbors down the road from them, the Skinners, who own a riding stable. Sam and I are allowed to go down there anytime we want to ride horses around their property. Sam never wants to go, though. She got on a horse once and whined so much that Mr. Skinner finally had to help her get down. And that was the oldest, slowest mare in the barn. The Skinners have a son my age named Tad. He and I ride together a lot, and we groom the horses and do other things that you have to do in a stable. And he collects baseball cards, too.

Not only do they live in a great place, Gram and Grandad are also a lot of fun themselves. I'd like to visit them no matter where they lived. Grandad is a neat guy who's really funny, sometimes even when he's not trying to be. He likes to do a lot of guy things with me that Dad doesn't always have time to do. He thinks it's important for a kid to learn useful things, like how to shoot a bow and arrow and how to chop wood for a fire without chopping your foot off.

Gram is a lot of fun, too. She makes desserts from scratch, right in her own kitchen, and—I can't help it—they taste a lot better than the desserts in paper cartons that Mom picks up at the Big Star Supermarket. Gram also makes the best popcorn and pours real butter on it, and she lets me stay up late to watch TV shows I've never even heard of. Gram belongs to this singing group called the Sweet Adelines. It's a bunch of ladies who get together and dress up in costumes and sing songs that only grandparents ever heard of. I went to a Sweet Adelines concert once that Gram sang in. I was real polite afterward and told her how it was very entertaining and everything. But I couldn't help thinking how the show could have been a lot better if only they had sung something by Michael Jackson or Paula Abdul. It would have been sensational to see those Adelines doing a little moon walking.

When we arrived at Gram and Grandad's, Dad and Mom helped us get settled in and unpacked. Mom reminded me about brushing my teeth every day and not picking on Samantha any more than absolutely necessary. Then she said, "Now Oliver, I know you want to find those old baseball cards of your father's, and Gram has said she'll help you look for them. But I don't want you to be too disappointed when you don't find them."

She and Dad looked at each other knowingly, thinking I didn't see them exchanging glances. I could tell they were pretty sure I didn't have a chance in the world of finding the cards.

"Don't worry," I said confidently. "I *am* going to find those cards. I just *know* it. I can *feel* that I'm going to find them. And I mean that, sincerely."

"Well, if you do," said Dad, "if you do happen to find them someplace, I want you to know that they'll be yours. After all your efforts, any baseball cards you find will belong to you. I hereby give up all claim to them. If you do happen to find this lost treasure, you deserve to own it."

"Wow! Thanks, Dad," I said, beaming happily. I was more determined than ever, now.

"Just don't drive your grandparents crazy or nag them to death," Dad warned. "You know how bullheaded you can be sometimes."

Me? Bullheaded? Determined, maybe, but I wouldn't exactly say "bullheaded" was an accurate description. That was a bit strong, I thought.

After Sam and I said our good-byes to Mom and Dad

(they had to kiss her Cabbage-Faces, too; can you believe it?), I started mapping out my strategy for the card search.

"This is going to be like looking for a needle in a haystack!" Grandad said. "Oliver, do you realize how much junk is packed away in this house? We have boxes and boxes of things in the attic and the basement. There are things in this house that I haven't seen since Hector was a pup!"

"Since *who* was a *what*?" I repeated, confused. Grandad didn't even *have* a dog.

"That's just an old saying," Grandad explained.

Oh, another one. There's an old saying for everything, according to Grandad. Any situation that comes up, Grandad has the perfect comment.

"You know what I mean," he went on. "There are just too many places to look. Something as small as baseball cards could be anywhere."

At that moment, Gram came into the room. She untied her apron and took it off.

"There's one thing I've always heard you say, Harry," she told Grandad. "You've said many a time that 'a journey of a thousand miles begins with a single step.' So, Oliver, let's start at the beginning and take that single step. How about if we start looking in your father's old room?"

All right, *Gram*!

The bedroom Dad had used when he was a kid is now a guest room. Gram and I started to look through the closet in that room, which was still crammed full of

Dad's old clothes, sports equipment, and other belongings. There were boots, skis, skates, tennis rackets, and all sorts of things I bet Dad doesn't even know he still has. Wow, I thought to myself. Dad yells at *me* for stuffing a lot of things into *my* closet. My closet looks like a drained swamp compared to this. On the top shelf of the closet was a stack of board games. I looked through each one of them, to make sure that no baseball cards had been carelessly mixed in with the game cards. That didn't turn up anything, but I set the Monopoly game out so that we could play later that evening.

Samantha came in and watched us searching the closet. She couldn't understand what the big deal was. She had never been able to see any sense at all in collecting baseball cards. But she's like a pet cat. You know how cats are—always curious about what's going on and always wanting to be in the middle of any activity. She propped her Cabbage-Face up on the bed so it could watch us (sure, Samantha) and proceeded to offer useless comments about what we were doing.

"I think this is a big waste of time" was her general opinion. "You're never going to find any old baseball cards. I think we should go down to the stable. I want to ride ponies this afternoon. Couldn't we please go riding, Gram? I really want to ride today." And of course, all this was said in that kind of whiny voice she does so well.

"Yeah, Samantha," I said. "This would be the one day in the whole history of the world that you want to

ride horses, the day that *I* want Gram to help me do something. Anyway, I doubt if they'll be able to find a horse down there that's slow enough for you. Maybe one that walks in its sleep."

"Now, now," said Gram. "Let's not make fun of Samantha, Oliver." She sighed, wearily, and started to fan herself with an old copy of *Boy's Life* from March 1958, which she'd taken out of the closet. As she fanned, I watched, astonished, as a small, flat, rectangular object flew from between the pages of the magazine and fluttered to the floor. It was a baseball card.

"Wow! Now we're getting somewhere!" I said excitedly. This was the beginning. Now I knew for certain that I was actually going to be able to find the lost collection!

I stooped to pick up the card and examined it eagerly. Vic Janowicz. Vic Janowicz? I couldn't really recall that name. Well, just because *I* had never heard of the guy didn't mean he wasn't important. I turned the card over and read Vic's stats on the reverse side. A utility man, lifetime batting average of 214. Played two seasons with the Pittsburgh Pirates.

Oh, well, so it wasn't the most outstanding card in the world. At least this meant that there were probably more cards where that one came from. I shook the copy of *Boy's Life* until I had made sure there was nothing more in there to fall out.

"It's so hot to be working like this," said Gram. "Let's go get some lemonade, and then maybe take Samantha's suggestion and go down to the riding stables."

"Gram!" I cried. "We can't quit now! Let's start looking up in the attic."

"The attic! In this heat?" Gram looked at me like I was crazy or something. "We'll wait till later on, Oliver. Maybe we'll take a look up there after the sun goes down, and it's not so blazing hot. Right now maybe we can do a few things with Samantha. We don't want her to feel neglected now, do we?"

Well, no. We certainly don't want *that*, for pete's sake. So we all trooped out to the front porch and Gram brought out lemonade and peanut butter cookies. Grandad had been out in the barn, getting his fishing gear in order, and he came over to have a snack with us. Then Gram and Grandad said they'd take us over to the Skinners' stable, just like Samantha wanted. How does such a little person manage to make everybody do exactly what she wants all the time? I wondered to myself. How does she do it?

I did have a good time at the stable, though, I have to admit. It was fun seeing Tad again. He showed me some of the new cards he'd collected since the last time I'd seen him and told me about a couple of card shows he'd been to. We rode horses around Tad's pasture and down some trails into the woods. Samantha actually got her horse going at a fast walk around the exercise ring. She was definitely making progress.

As she had promised, Gram went up to the attic with me as soon as the sun went down to continue the search. To speed things along, I helped her clean up the dishes after dinner. I worked faster than I ever had and didn't

drop a single glass. She was impressed. We finished up in the kitchen; then Gram and I climbed the steep ladder that led to the attic and had a look around.

"What a mess!" said Gram, looking at the cluttered attic space. "I forgot how much junk was up here."

There were boxes everywhere, more boxes than I'd ever seen in one place in my life. And on top of the boxes were lamps, umbrella stands, tricycles, sleds, picture frames, and just about anything else you could think of. I was starting to believe that my grandmother had never thrown away anything in her entire life. And that gave me even more hope that we would eventually find Dad's lost cards. If Gram had never thrown anything away, then it wasn't likely that she would have thrown those cards away, either. That only made sense.

"This is impossible!" exclaimed Gram. "Oliver, do you realize what you're asking me to do? It's possible—not probable, but possible—that I saved those cards. But I might have put them in a little box and packed the little box into one of those big boxes. We could search for days through all this stuff and never find any cards. If you ask me, I think we should forget the whole thing. I'll take you down to Save Mart tomorrow and buy you ten packs of new cards. Just don't ask me to look through all these boxes!"

Oh, no! Gram was wimping out. I looked at her with the most gloomy, disappointed expression I could muster up. I tried to think of the saddest thing I possibly could. I thought about Jose Canseco being traded to the Cleveland Indians. I imagined that they had just announced that summer vacation was to be shortened by four weeks. I thought about how I'd feel if the dentist told Mom I'd have to wear my retainer for the rest of my life. The expression on my face must have been the saddest one Gram had ever seen in her life. And it worked!

"Oh, all right," she said, finally. "Maybe going through the attic will give me a chance to get rid of some of this old stuff we don't need anymore." She glanced around the attic and shook her head. "There's enough material here for about ten garage sales. Or maybe I should just gather up all these things and take them to Goodwill. All right, Oliver, we'll search the attic. That sad face of yours has gotten to me, just like you hoped it would."

"YES!" I cried. "YES, Gram! You're the greatest! And I mean that, sincerely!"

And I did.

CHAPTER 3

So Gram and I started on the attic. She had a grim expression on her face and vowed that she would spend only half an hour that night wading through the sea of boxes. She told me she wanted to go to bed at a reasonable time.

I was happy that my sad face had worked its charm and that I hadn't had to resort to nagging her into helping me search. Although, I must admit, I've accomplished a lot in life through nagging and am probably a world-class nagger. Not as good as Samantha, though.

We decided to take it one box at a time. Gram opened the first box by slitting the masking tape with a little paring knife, and we were on our way. We *were* going to find those long lost baseball cards; I was sure of it.

Four hours later, I was starting to get a little discouraged.

By then, it was after nine o'clock. Sam had long since gone to bed and was probably in Cabbage-Face dreamland. Grandad was stretched out, sound asleep, in his reclining chair in front of the television. There was a Cubs game on the tube, in the seventh inning, but Grandad was oblivious to it. Gram and I had opened and looked through about fifteen cartons of what seemed to me to be a lot of junk. Gram called it memorabilia. *She* seemed to be having the time of her life. She was finding things she hadn't seen in years and didn't even remember she had. She found a recipe box that she hadn't seen since Eisenhower was president. She found an old, green velvet hat with a veil. It had gone out of style, she said, but had been in the attic so long that it was probably back in style by now. She wiped the dust from an old mirror and tried that hat on. She had also found a large box of Dad's old clothes from when he was a kid.

"These clothes are in such good condition," she said, pulling some of them out of the box. The overwhelming smell of mothballs just about knocked me out. She held up a sort of plaid shirt that, believe me, only a nerd would wear. "And madras is coming back into style, they say." Madras shirts. Sad to think my own father would wear something like that. I fervently hoped that my dad had not been a nerd.

"You know, *you* could probably wear some of these clothes, Oliver," Gram said.

I groaned inside. Yeah, I thought to myself, and then

I could play with a Hula Hoop and listen to Chubby Checker records. Out loud I said, "Yeah, Gram, that would be great, and I sure would like to try on some of those neat clothes sometime, but—"

"But not right now, right?" asked Gram.

"Right," I agreed. "I'd like to save that for later in the week." When I *really* want to start having fun, I added to myself. "Right now, let's look in a couple more of these boxes, okay?"

"No, I don't think so. Not tonight," said Gram. "It's getting late, and I've had it with this dusty attic. We'll get some sleep and have another look tomorrow." She had a that's-final tone to her voice, so I didn't even bother nagging her. I could see she meant what she said. I only hoped that, once she left the attic, I could persuade her to go back up there again to continue the search.

We made our way carefully back down the steep ladder. Gram made some popcorn; I think she felt sorry for me and wanted to make up a little for my disappointment in not finding what I wanted in the attic. Together we watched an old Humphrey Bogart movie about a detective who was pretty cool, named Sam Spade. In the movie, a whole bunch of people were trying to get this treasure, an old bird statue, which in the end turned out to be not worth anything after all. I thought about how I was on sort of a treasure hunt, too. Only my treasure was definitely going to be worth finding in the end.

♦

The next morning, Gram fixed a big breakfast for us. She called it a farm breakfast. There were pancakes with syrup, home fries (something Sam and I hadn't tasted before), biscuits dripping with butter, a platter of bacon, and lots of scrambled eggs. Sam and I are used to having a bowl of Fruit Loops in the morning with a glass of orange juice, so we were pretty well stuffed after that meal. I guess after eating a breakfast like that you're supposed to feel like plowing a couple of fields or milking a few cows or something. All I felt like doing was lying down in front of the television.

"Well, come on, Oliver," said Gram as she finished up the dishes and took off her apron. "If you want to finish searching the attic, let's go to it before it starts getting really hot up there."

I instantly forgot about my full stomach and raced up the ladder to the attic, with Gram behind me, going at a slightly slower pace.

Unfortunately, we went through every remaining box that was up there without turning up a thing. Not one baseball card. Not even another Vic Janowicz. The closest we came to finding anything even related to baseball was an old scrapbook with pasted-in ticket stubs from a 1962 Cincinnati Reds game. Apparently Grandad and Dad had gone to that game, and that was kind of interesting. But I was really disappointed about not finding one single baseball card.

"Gram," I pleaded, "please try to think. Isn't there

anywhere else—anyplace at all—that you might have stored some other things?"

Gram sighed and sat down on an overturned wicker basket. She started to fan herself with another old magazine, this time a copy of something called *Look*. It was from 1960 and had a picture of John F. Kennedy and his wife, Jackie, on the cover. Gram studied the cover photo intently.

"I used to have a pillbox hat just like that," she said. "I wonder whatever happened to it."

"Gram," I said again. "Please try to think. Where else could we look?"

"Well, there are a few boxes and things in the basement," she said. "Not many, but—"

"All right!" I cried. "Let's go!"

"Now, Oliver, really! Don't get excited, because there are just a few things down there—" She fanned herself again. "And I'm going to rest a bit," she added. She leaned back and opened up her 1960 copy of *Look* magazine.

I was already halfway down the stairs to the basement. Gram was right; there weren't too many interesting things down there. The basement was mostly used as a laundry room. There were clothes baskets, piles of laundry, an ironing board, things like that. But Grandad had built some floor-to-ceiling wooden shelves against one wall, and the shelves were stacked with boxes. Boxes! My favorite thing.

I called Grandad to help me take down some of the boxes from the shelves. He did, but made me promise that, after inspecting each box, I would replace the contents neatly, leaving everything the way I found it. For the next few hours, I searched thoroughly through every box. They were filled with things like old record albums, income tax records, and books; nothing too interesting.

After I'd been working for a while, Gram came to the top of the basement stairs and called down to me.

"Oliver!" she said. "I hate for you to be down in that damp, dark basement all morning when it's such a beautiful day outside. I really would rather you come up here and go outdoors to play. Samantha wants you to go fishing with her; I think it would be nice if you'd do something with your little sister for a while."

Doesn't anyone understand? I thought gloomily. I was hot on the trail of a baseball card treasure, and no one thought it was important but me. No one could see the value in what I was trying to do. Couldn't they understand how exciting it would be to find and brush the dust off a 1959 Al Kaline? Didn't they know that those baseball cards had to be here, somewhere, right under our noses? And I knew Samantha didn't want me to go fishing with her because she enjoyed the pleasure of my company, for pete's sake. She just wanted me to go down to the lake with her so I could put the bait on her hook. She loves to fish, all right. As long as she doesn't have to touch anything slimy.

As I was sitting there on the basement floor, feeling very misunderstood, I happened to glance up to the top shelf of boxes. Right above the top shelf was a rafter.

And sitting on that rafter, back against the basement ceiling, almost completely out of sight, was what looked like a school book bag. And the book bag had a picture on it. I jumped up and climbed on top of one of the biggest cartons, trying to get a closer look. No . . . Could it really be? It was a picture of Fred Flintstone! Yes, it was definitely Fred! I suddenly felt like that movie detective Sam Spade, finding an important clue. Dad had told me he carried his baseball cards to and from school in his Flintstones book bag. Could he have possibly left them there? Could the cards have been safely tucked away in that old book bag all these years?

"Grandad!" I yelled excitedly. "Grandad, *help*!"

Grandad appeared at the top of the basement stairs in about five seconds flat. I hadn't known he could move that fast.

"Oliver! Are you okay?" he asked anxiously.

"Grandad, come down here, please!" I yelled. "You've got to get a ladder and help me get Fred Flintstone down!"

Grandad was confused. "Fred Flintstone? What's he doing down there?"

But when he figured out what I really wanted, and I explained quickly about the Flintstones book bag being used to transport baseball cards, Grandad got sort of excited, too. He got the ladder, climbed up to the top shelf, and retrieved the battered old book bag. It was covered with dust from having sat on that rafter a long time without being moved. Grandad brushed some of the dust off and sneezed violently several times. Then he carefully came back down the ladder and proudly handed me the Flintstones book bag.

"There you are, Oliver," he said happily. "I hope there's a big surprise in there for you."

I was so excited I could hardly make my fingers unbuckle the straps that closed the bag. Finally, after a tense minute or two, I got the bag open and looked inside. The book bag was crammed full of all sorts of things, papers, mostly. I dumped the contents of the bag on the cement floor of the basement and spread everything out in front of me. I looked anxiously through the pile for something, anything, that looked like a baseball card.

No luck. There was nothing that even remotely resembled a baseball card. Not even one.

I noticed there were a couple of pockets and zippered compartments. I opened each zipper, still hoping I might find something. I groped around in each pocket, but again, no luck.

I was too disappointed for words. I just sat there on the basement floor, feeling miserable. Of course, I wasn't about to cry or anything like that, but I did start getting this lump in the back of my throat that felt like it was about the size of the state of Montana. And I could suddenly feel that big farm breakfast I had eaten, sitting there like a bowling ball in the pit of my stomach.

Grandad didn't know what to say. He knew I felt pretty bad. Then he thought for a moment and suddenly came up with something he felt suited the occasion.

"Well, it was a good try. And, you know, Oliver, if at first you don't succeed, try, try, again."

"Try what?" I asked dejectedly. It was difficult to get the words out with that big lump stuck in my throat. My voice sounded thinner and squeakier than it usually does. "We've looked everywhere there is to look."

"Well, maybe if we think real hard, we'll be able to come up with something else." Grandad was a pretty optimistic guy. He went on, "How would you like to go into town with me while I run some errands? We'll stop at Larson's and get this week's copy of that baseball card magazine you like. And then we can go to Dairy Delite and get a chocolate sundae with nuts. How does that sound, Ollie?"

"Thanks, Grandad," I said glumly. He was trying to make me feel better, and I appreciated that. "That would be fun, I guess."

Samantha wanted to go with us, of course. She never likes to miss out on a single thing, even if it's something that she wouldn't enjoy that much. Gram convinced her to stay home with her, saying they could have a lot more fun making a peach pie. Gram told her she'd teach her how to peel peaches. That didn't sound like a whole lot of fun to me, but Samantha had never peeled peaches before, so she was easily convinced.

♦

That evening, the four of us sat in the den and watched an old rerun of the "I Love Lucy" show. I love Lucy, the show, I mean, and one of my favorite episodes was on.

As we watched, I opened Dad's old book bag again, and spread the papers out on the floor to have another look. Maybe I'd come up with a clue of some kind that might tell me something about what had happened to the baseball card collection.

It was interesting to look at Dad's old school papers from a hundred years ago. Well, not a hundred years, exactly, but it seems like that to me. Dad always says it seems like it was only yesterday that he was a kid in school. But the way he tells it, things were really backward then. It seems like it must have been a hundred years ago.

I picked up a science test that Dad had taken. It had a big red F on it, with a circle around it. The teacher had written, in red ink, "You were not prepared!!!" Wow, three exclamation points. I couldn't imagine my dad actually flunking a test. To hear him tell it, he was little Mister Perfect, the teacher's pet. He never actually said he was the teacher's pet, but from what he did say, that was the general impression I got.

There were several old comic books in the bag, ones I'd never heard of. There was this little ghost dude named Casper, and another one about this little girl witch, who looked like what a Cabbage-Face would look like if it got a little older. Her name was Little Itch. Cute. Pretty hilarious stuff, I thought, shaking my head in disbelief as I thumbed through the comics. My own dad used to read this cornball stuff. The price of ten cents was printed on the cover of each comic book. That was hard to believe, too.

"I don't know why there would be comic books in that book bag," said Gram disapprovingly. She looked over my shoulder as I leafed through the Casper comic. "I know for a *fact* that I never let your father take comic books to school."

I examined a bubble gum wrapper that had once contained baseball cards. Now it was empty, without a trace of the cards it had once been wrapped around. I wondered which ones they had been. There were also some old handwritten notes on lined paper. One note was from some girl named Kathy. It was what you would call sort of an admiring letter, and it made me just about hoot with laughter. I could picture my dad, the really cool-dude-about-school, with his madras shirt and Flintstones book bag, with all the babes hanging around his locker.

"What's so funny, Oliver?" asked Grandad, noticing the kind of smirky grin on my face as I visualized Dad in all his junior high glory.

"Uh . . . uh, Lucy," I stammered. "This is my favorite part, where she bites that wax fruit."

"That was five minutes ago," Grandad pointed out. "You're still laughing?"

I continued to look through Dad's papers. There was another handwritten note, this one from a boy, a friend of Dad's, apparently, named Jake. The note said, "Henry—" (Henry is my dad's name; can you believe it?) "Henry—I got a new pack of Star Players. I got a

Willie Mays. Trade your Brooks Robinson? Meet you later at the clubhouse. When Mr. Slocum says the word *homework*, we're all going to drop our history books."

Boy, Dad was really the model student, I thought to myself. Passing notes, reading comic books, tormenting teachers. Looking at your father's old book bag can be very revealing. Even *I* don't take comic books to school. I'd get killed for that kind of stuff.

"How about trying some of these on, Oliver?" Gram asked. She had a box that she'd brought down from the attic, full of Dad's old clothes. She was making two stacks: one of clothes she wanted me to try on; the other was clothing she was going to take to Goodwill because she already knew it wouldn't fit me. She held up a fuzzy sweater that was a shade of fish-pond green you don't see too often these days. It looked like something Elvis Presley would have worn in one of his early movies.

"Look at this beautiful mohair sweater," Gram said. "It hardly looks worn at all. Try it on, Oliver. That color will be wonderful on you."

If I were a frog that color might look good on me, I thought. Out loud I said, "I wonder how many mo's they had to kill to make that sweater." I started laughing really hard at my little joke. Gram and Grandad didn't think it was nearly as funny as I did, and they just kind of looked at me blankly. Samantha looked confused, but that was to be expected.

"I'll try it on later," I promised. Maybe by the time later rolled around, Gram would have forgotten all about it. That sweater definitely looked like the kind that would itch, and I really didn't want to get too close to it. "I'll try on clothes tomorrow," I assured her again.

"Okay," said Gram. "But remember, you promised." She smiled cheerfully and folded up the mohair sweater. "Anyone for fresh peach pie?" she asked. "The peaches were peeled personally by Samantha O'Malley."

Sounded great to me. I had a huge slice of warm pie with a big, slurpy scoop of french vanilla ice cream on top. Samantha beamed proudly, like she had invented peach pie or something, instead of just peeling the peaches. However, I wisely kept myself from making any smart remarks about her efforts. And I have to admit it, that peach pie was pretty delicious.

"And tomorrow," said Sam, "guess what? We're going to shuck corn!"

Boy, I thought, in my book that certainly tops peeling peaches for having a whale of a good time.

Grandad and I had already decided that we were going to take the boat out on the lake and do some serious fishing the next day. No girls allowed. Now, that sounded like *my* idea of having a good time. I asked for a second helping of pie and started planning my strategy for catching a big fish. I was able to forget, for a while anyway, my frustrating search for the lost baseball cards.

The next morning, Samantha was already in the kitchen doing her baking thing by the time I got up. Half asleep, I stumbled downstairs, sat down at the kitchen table, and watched her in action. She was rolling out dough for sourdough biscuits with a big, wooden rolling pin. She looked like she actually knew what she was doing. And she seemed to be getting a major kick out of it. Boy, am I ever glad I'm not a girl. And I mean that, sincerely.

A short time after we'd had our breakfast (another farm breakfast), the phone rang. From what Grandad was saying, I could tell it was Dad on the other end. After speaking to Dad for a few minutes, Grandad handed the telephone to me.

"Your father wants to talk to you, Oliver," he said.

Dad told me that he and Mom were having the time

of their lives. He said they had gone to some really terrific gourmet restaurants, had seen an exhibit of post-modern collages (whatever *they* are) at the Guggenheim Museum, and had had tea at the Plaza Hotel. That didn't sound to me like such a rip-roaring good time. If *I* had gone to New York City, I would have gone to the Statue of Liberty, the Hard Rock Cafe, and of course, a Yankees game. But you know how parents are; they like all that really boring stuff.

Anyway, I told Dad about finding his Flintstones book bag and about looking at his school papers and notes from his classmates. He didn't seem real comfortable about me looking through his old school stuff, and I could kind of see why. I hadn't planned to bring up the subject of the science test, but I couldn't help myself.

"Hey, Dad, there was a science test in with all this stuff, which apparently you flunked. I didn't know you used to flunk tests."

"Never mind, Oliver," said Dad. "I may have gotten an F once or twice in my life. I'm sure that if I failed a test, there was a perfectly good explanation."

"There was a note in there, too," I went on, "from a kid named Jake. It was all about how he wanted you to trade some baseball cards with him. He said in the note that he'd meet you at the clubhouse after school. Did you have a clubhouse, Dad?"

Dad paused a moment to think. "Why, yes, Oliver," he said. "Gosh, I'd forgotten all about our old clubhouse. It was way out in the woods, pretty far from the house, as I remember. All my friends went there and hung out. We sort of had a little baseball card club, actually. The clubhouse was really an old toolshed that Grandad wasn't using. We kids kind of took it over and made it into our headquarters. Imagine that. After all these years, I'd totally forgotten."

When you've lived as many years as Dad has, you're bound to forget a few minor details. But to forget a whole *clubhouse*, for pete's sake? If I had had a clubhouse, it would have been a major thing in my life, a big enough thing that I'm sure I would have mentioned it to my own family once or twice.

"Where exactly was this clubhouse, Dad?" I asked.

"Well, like I said, way, way out in the woods, up near one of the pastures, I think. Your grandfather would know where it was." Dad paused again, as if he were trying to remember something. "Hey, Oliver," he said. "You know, if you're still looking for those old baseball cards of mine, you might want to look around and see if that old shed is still there. I used to keep my card collection in the clubhouse. I had a padlock for the door, and I kept a lot of my things out there. Who knows? There might still be something there, although I don't know what kind of condition any cards might be in by now."

I thought of that kid in New England who had found the Honus Wagner card. That card had been found in a box buried in dirt for all these years. So why couldn't cards be found inside an abandoned shed? I found myself getting excited about my search again.

I hardly heard anything else Dad was saying to me,

I was so busy thinking about his clubhouse. When my mother got on the phone to say a few words, I know my conversation was a little vague.

"Oliver," she said, "are you remembering to brush your teeth?"

"Uh, yeah, Mom. I'm doing fine. How about you?"

"Are you wearing your retainer every day?"

"Yeah, Mom, I miss you, too."

Then Mom and Dad said they missed Samantha and wanted to speak to her, too. What did they miss about Samantha? I wondered. Her whining, maybe. I called the little angel to the phone and went to get my fishing gear. Grandad was ready to go and was waiting for me. Gram had packed us a picnic lunch to take along. The basket was bulging with sandwiches and fruit, enough to feed us for about two weeks. Grandad started up the motor on the boat, and we took off to find the best fishing spot possible. On this particular day, it was a shady spot in a little lagoon, on the other side of the lake. When we got to the perfect place, Grandad shut off the motor, and we dropped our lines into the water. As soon as we were settled, Grandad opened the picnic basket and took out a large turkey and provolone sandwich.

"Isn't it a little early for lunch?" I asked, watching him take a huge bite out of the sandwich.

He shook his head vigorously. "No time like the present, Ollie boy."

"Grandad," I said, "I was asking Dad about the clubhouse he used to have when he was a kid. It was an old toolshed, he says. Do you remember anything about it?"

"Sure," said Grandad, between bites. "Henry and his friends used that clubhouse for years. You're right; it was an old toolshed that I wasn't using for anything. Years ago, and I mean a lot of years, like forty or fifty, there was a stable out there and some other small outbuildings. But they burned down—I forget why or how. The toolshed was way out in that pasture all by itself, so I really didn't have occasion to use it ever. I built another toolshed, closer to the barn and told the boys they could have the old shed to play in."

"What happened to that toolshed?" I asked. "Is it still out there?"

"Well, I guess so. I certainly didn't do anything to it," Grandad said as he started in on a big, juicy, red apple. "As far as I know, it's still there. I haven't seen that old shed in years. Probably covered over in leaves and growth by now."

I was getting really excited about the turn of events but tried to remain calm as I announced, "Grandad. We've got to find that shed and see if the baseball cards are out there."

Grandad stopped, midbite. "We do?" he asked, looking doubtful.

"You've *got* to show me where the clubhouse is. You've got to help me find it."

"I do?" said Grandad. From the pained expression on his face, I could see that searching the woods for

Dad's old clubhouse was probably number one on his top ten list of things he did not want to do.

"Please!" I said. "Pleeeeeeeeease, Grandad! You've just got to. Those valuable baseball cards might be out there in the clubhouse, or toolshed, or whatever it is, just waiting for someone to discover them. Just waiting for *us* to discover them. Please, Grandad."

"But, Oliver," said Grandad reasonably, "it's been years. Those cards couldn't have lasted out there all this time. Someone would have found them. I'm positive they're not still there."

"But maybe they *are*, Grandad," I cried. It occurred to me suddenly that my voice was sounding dangerously close to a Samantha-type whine, so I lowered it a little. "Please, you've just got to help me. Finding those cards would make me the happiest kid in the state of Ohio. Maybe even in the whole continental U.S.A. It wouldn't take that long to walk out there, would it? How far can it be?"

"Pretty far," Grandad told me. "On a three-hundred-acre farm, you can walk quite a distance, you know. And it's hot. And we might not even be able to find that old shed, even if we searched all day. And if we do find it, I bet you dollars to doughnuts that there's absolutely nothing inside but a couple of spiders."

"Okay," I said glumly. This time I didn't have to imagine summer vacation being cut short, or any other sad thing, in order to get a downcast expression on my face. After all the hard work and searching I had done so far, it seemed so unfair not to be able to look any further for the baseball cards when I knew almost for certain where they were.

Grandad looked up at the sky, so he didn't have to look at my sad face. After a minute or two of silence, he said, "Oliver, you know something? You're spoiling your whole visit with us because of this baseball card thing. You can't have any fun while you're constantly worried about those cards. If they're not around anymore, then they're not around. There's not much you can do about it. Your grandmother and I have helped you all we can, but I think it's about time to throw in the towel. And I think you've got something on your line."

Startled at the abrupt change in subject, I looked up at my pole. It was bent over the side of the boat, and the bobber was nowhere in sight. I quickly started to reel in what felt like a twelve-pound bass. When I finally got the wild, fighting largemouth into the boat, it looked a lot more like a two-pounder. Nevertheless, I had made the first catch of the day. And as it turned out, the last.

"Great job!" yelled Grandad, slapping me on the back. "You handled that like a pro, Oliver! That big fish didn't have a chance! You were great. I'm really proud of you. And," he said, "you know what they say, Ollie boy."

"No, Grandad." I smiled. "What do they say?"

"The early bird catches the worm!"

"What does *that* mean?" I asked him. I mean, I knew what it meant, basically. But I didn't understand how it had anything to do with catching that fish. Sometimes Grandad's sayings were more confusing than enlightening.

"That means," said Grandad, "that we're going to have to get up real early tomorrow morning if we're going to spend the day looking for that clubhouse."

The clubhouse! Now there was a big smile on my face. Grandad wasn't going to let me down after all.

"Thanks, Grandad!" I said. "You're the greatest! And," I added, "I mean that, sincerely."

"Just promise me one thing, though," Grandad said. "If I take you out there, and we find the clubhouse, you've got to promise me something. If the cards aren't there—and they probably aren't—you have to promise that you'll forget all about them, and that you'll just relax and enjoy the rest of your vacation."

"Okay," I assured him. "No problem. If the cards aren't there, then I guarantee it—I won't mention them again. And I mean that, too, sincerely."

♦

The next morning, we had another one of those big breakfasts, this time with poached eggs and ham. In this case, we really needed to eat a big meal. Grandad and I were going to need a lot of energy for our long hike across the fields and farmland in search of the missing clubhouse. Samantha had made (with a *lot* of help from Gram) some blueberry muffins. They really looked delicious. I couldn't wait to taste one. They looked moist and crumbly, just like the picture in the cookbook Sam showed me. But when I bit into one, I found that I had to chew each bite for about three minutes before I could swallow it. It felt like a tennis ball going down. When Grandad and I left the house, Gram was still trying to figure out which ingredient Sam had forgotten to put in.

Grandad and I set off with a large backpack, which held candy bars, a compass so we wouldn't get lost, and a few small tools that Grandad thought might come in handy. He guessed that we should start out heading toward the north pasture. We hiked past the big vegetable garden. We walked by two cornfields, and then we made our way through a small patch of woods. After the woods, we came to a creek, which was too wide to jump across. We had to take off our shoes and wade. After that, Grandad wanted to sit down and rest for a while. I didn't want to stop; I was anxious to get on with our expedition. But I knew he was tired, so I sat down with him. We ended up eating every single candy bar that was in our backpack, which I didn't think was such a great idea. After all, we were only twenty minutes from home. We had just started our journey, and now all the provisions were gone. I started worrying that we would get lost for days in the woods, and that we'd starve to death. But Grandad didn't seem too worried about that happening.

"It's been a long time since I walked these fields," he said as we trudged along. That same nostalgic expression that I see on Dad a lot suddenly came across Grandad's face. "I haven't been back in these woods since your father was a boy," he went on. "You know, we just might find that toolshed in pretty good condition. It was built pretty solidly. I can't imagine it just blowing over in a storm or anything. Of course, vandals might have happened by, and set fire to it or something, but . . ."

"But we're never going to know unless we get out there and find it," I reminded him a little impatiently. "After all, Grandad, you know what they say, don't you?"

"What's that, Oliver?"

"He who hesitates is lost."

Grandad's eyes got pretty wide at that. "Well, now, Oliver," he said, standing up, "that's a pretty good one. He who hesitates is lost. I haven't heard that one in a month of Sundays."

Grandad and I walked on, across a large potato field and through another field that was overgrown with wildflowers and tall grass. The sun was directly overhead now, so I knew it must be close to noon. We'd been walking a pretty long time, and it was getting really hot. I took a pair of sunglasses from my back pocket and put them on.

"Hmm. Movie star, huh?" was Grandad's comment. Then he stopped abruptly and looked straight ahead, shading his eyes with his hand.

"Those woods over there," he said, pointing west. "That's where the clubhouse was, I think. In those woods over there."

I looked in the direction he was pointing. There was a dense thicket of trees in the distance.

"I'm sure of it," Grandad said. "Let's see." He checked the compass again. "That's west, so that must be the right set of woods. Let's go investigate. Come on, Hollywood."

We made our way toward the woods and then into them. It was difficult to walk through the thick tangle of branches and vines and bushes. There wasn't a path, so we sort of had to make one as we went along. Every few seconds, I glanced cautiously down to my feet to make sure I didn't step on any snakes. In all the time I'd been visiting Gram and Grandad, which was all my life, really, I had never seen a single snake. But I always expected to. And I figured I was due. I could also already feel the chigger bites I knew I was going to have after this adventure. But it would be worth it, I was certain of that.

Eventually, our efforts paid off. After a lot of scratches from thorny bushes and getting slapped in the face by prickly branches, Grandad suddenly hollered, "Here it is!"

And there it was. It was a little shack, not tiny, but not real big, either. It was sturdily built, with a raised wooden floor. There were two steps up to the front door, and on that door was a big, old, rusty padlock.

"This is it!" said Grandad triumphantly. The clubhouse was still standing, after all. But it was so overgrown with bushes and vines that you could hardly get a really good look at it. Grandad took a tool he had brought along, which he called a machete, and cut away some of the branches that covered the front door. I could see that it was one of the best kid clubhouses I had ever seen, even all covered over the way it was. Boy, I could really have fun with a little clubhouse like that. It could be a fort, a jail, a castle—anything you wanted it to be. I could think of a hundred different games you could play with a clubhouse like that.

But now I really wanted to see the inside of it. I looked uncertainly at the lock on the tightly shut door. But Grandad said, "Now that's why I brought along my handy-dandy all-purpose saw." He took a small hacksaw from the backpack and began to saw steadily. After a minute or so, the padlock broke apart into two pieces. I think it had been almost ready to disintegrate because of all the rust. I nudged the door open apprehensively; who could tell what was going to be inside? I was almost afraid to look. I peeked around the edge of the door. It was dark in there, and I couldn't see much. I disregarded the goose bumps on my arms and stepped cautiously inside.

It smelled terrible in there, all moldy and musty, like the worst damp basement you've ever been in, only ten times worse than that. There were two windows in the clubhouse, with glass panes, but vines and branches had grown over them, so there was hardly any light. Grandad handed me a flashlight from his backpack, and I beamed the light around the inside of the little structure. I saw a small table and the two old-fashioned wooden folding chairs. On the table I could see a few items, which I tried to identify. One was a Flintstones lunch box, very rusty. Then there was a threadbare catcher's mitt, which had definitely seen better days. On the little table were a couple of round objects, which I thought might be some ancient Oreo cookies. I couldn't be sure, because they were green and kind of fuzzy. There was a small, round, tin box with a combination lock on it. The box had a picture of a ball and bat on the lid and the words *Cincinnati Reds—1961* in big red letters. I picked up the box and shook it gently. There was definitely something inside, and the something felt like it could possibly be baseball cards!

"What's going on, Oliver?" Grandad was still standing in the doorway of the clubhouse, peering anxiously inside.

"It's a box, Grandad," I said, holding it up to show him. "A little tin box that would be a perfect place to keep your favorite baseball cards. Look!"

I tried to pry open the lid to the box, but couldn't manage it. I took the box over to where Grandad was, where there was more daylight.

"Do you think you could saw this lock off?" I asked, showing it to him up close. "I bet you anything there's something in here."

Grandad shook the box, too. "Certainly sounds promising," he said. He set the box down and began working on it with his hacksaw. The little combination lock wasn't as rusty as the padlock on the door had been, so it was going to take a little longer.

While he worked, I examined more closely the other objects on the table. The Flintstones lunch box was empty, except for an old drinking straw. Boy, Dad really had a thing for those Flintstones, I thought to myself. And the catcher's mitt. I'll bet Dad had used that in a lot of Little League games. The glove was for a left-hander, and Dad was left-handed, so I figured the glove had probably belonged to him. I decided I'd take it home with me and give it to him. He would enjoy seeing it again, I was sure. The antique cookies, I decided, didn't need further examination, although my science teacher might have been interested in them.

Just then, Grandad broke open the lock. He lifted the lid of the little tin box and peered inside.

"Cards!" he cried. "Cards, Oliver!"

My heart started pounding with excitement. That was it!

Then he said, "Uh-oh!"

"What? What?" I said, trying to look over his shoulder into the box. They were cards, all right. Grandad took the cards out of the box and laid them on the little table. They were bubble gum cards; the wrappers were still inside the tin box, too. But they were the wrong kind of bubble gum cards. The goofy faces of Larry, Moe, and Curly smiled up at me from the top card. The Three Stooges, for gosh sake! These guys had never played major league baseball! I quickly shuffled through all the cards, hoping that maybe some baseball cards had gotten mixed in with the Three Stooges. Nope. Every card had a photo of the Stooges, doing one stupid thing after another. Every single one.

The state of Montana started growing in my throat again. This time I couldn't speak at all. I just stared sorrowfully at the little tin box. My last hope.

"Well," said Grandad. "I guess that's it. Back to the drawing board, right, Ollie boy?"

Easy for you to say, I thought, feeling really defeated. I knew I would never find those baseball cards now. This was the last place they could have been. I had been so sure that we'd find them in the clubhouse. It had seemed so perfect. I was starting to realize that it was probably true; the Willie Mays rookie card and the 1958 Whitey Ford *were* at the bottom of a landfill somewhere.

"So near, and yet so far," said Grandad thoughtfully. "That's the way the cookie crumbles, I guess. But keep your chin up, Oliver. It's not the end of the world."

I stirred my green beans around on my dinner plate. Grandad just didn't understand. No one understood how badly I had wanted those cards. Everyone felt sorry for me, though, even Samantha. She tried to cheer me up by telling me the entire plot of an old Shirley Temple movie she'd seen on TV that morning. She didn't just tell the story, either; she had to show me how Shirley tap-danced and sang, "On the go-oo-oood ship *Lollipop*, it's a swee-ee-eet trip to the candy shop." She seemed to think this movie was really hilarious, for some reason. I don't think it was actually supposed to be a comedy. Samantha's sense of humor seems to me to be out of step with the rest of the world. She always thinks stories about lost dogs and orphans and things like that are supposed to be funny. Then she'll watch one of the funniest "I Love Lucy" shows and stare at the television real seriously, like it was some kind of a doorknob or something, like she couldn't understand what was so funny about it. With Lucy, I think it's pretty obvious why it's funny. You don't have to be a real deep thinker or anything to figure it out.

Anyway, I didn't feel much like eating, with everyone sitting there with these real pitying expressions on their faces. Gram had made a chocolate cake for dessert. I could tell Sam had had a hand in putting the icing on, because there was this lopsided happy face drawn in yellow on the top of the cake. It looked pretty dumb, but I had a piece of cake, anyway. For one thing, I knew Sam's feelings would be hurt if I didn't have a bite of her happy face, and for another, it looked like pretty good cake.

"Hey, I just thought of a great idea," said Grandad, stopping with a forkful of cake midway to his mouth.

We all looked at him expectantly.

"I think I know where I can get four tickets to a Cincinnati Reds baseball game. How about that? Would you all like to go?"

Would I like to go? Would Nolan Ryan like to pitch a perfect game? Would Reggie Jackson have liked to hit sixty-two home runs in a season? Would Pete Rose like to be in the Hall of Fame? The only not-so-great part of Grandad's idea was that I assumed he was including Samantha in the foursome that would be going to the game. For a chance to see the Cincinnati Reds play, live and in person, though, I could even put up with that. As long as we didn't have to get tickets for any of the Cabbage-Faces.

The game was on Friday, and Grandad came through with the tickets as promised. As it turned out, he had a friend who had a friend who knew somebody who had tickets for some swell seats right behind home plate. We had to drive two hours to get to Cincinnati, but it wasn't too bad; I got to sit in the front seat with Grandad. Gram and Samantha sat in the backseat and played Go Fish most of the way. That's Sam's favorite card game; well, actually, it's her only card game. She loves those intellectual challenges. Grandad and I, in the front seat, had more important things to talk about, like batting averages, home run leaders, and who we thought was going to win the pennant that year.

It was a fantastic experience, being at a real, live professional baseball game, even better than I had imagined it would be. It was a night game, which I thought made it even more exciting. It was like being in a movie, almost; the colors were brighter, the popcorn tasted better, the organ music coming out of the sound system was loud and clear; it added just the right touch of atmosphere. I had brought Dad's catcher's mitt with me, the one I had found in the clubhouse. I wanted to be ready in case any balls were hit out into the crowd. I figured Dad's old glove would bring me luck. Wow, would it ever be fantastic to catch a souvenir ball, hit by one of my favorite players. I kept the mitt on the whole time, ready to catch the ball that happened to come into the stands.

We bought cotton candy, hot dogs, popcorn, root beer, and souvenirs. Samantha got a Reds pennant, and I got a baseball cap. I decided then and there that that cap was going to be my trademark, my signature. I was never going to take it off, except for sleeping. Maybe not even then. From the first few notes of the "Star-Spangled Banner" to the last exciting moments, when the Reds pulled the game out four to three, it was the most fun I had ever had.

There were only two minor mishaps during the game, which I'll mention, but I didn't really let them spoil the game for me.

The first one happened when the Reds scored their first run. I got so excited and was yelling my head off so frantically that my retainer got jarred loose somehow and fell out of my mouth. Which wouldn't have been so bad, except that it fell down the back of the jacket of a guy who was sitting in front of me. This guy was already not too happy with us, because we were cheering so hard for the Reds and he was a fan of the team they were beating. He had to unzip his jacket and take it off so I could get my retainer back. When he saw what had fallen into his jacket, he was totally grossed out. He was pretty mad, but the other people sitting around us thought it was hilarious.

The second thing that happened was this: As I told you, I was sitting there the whole time with Dad's glove on, ready to catch any foul balls that came my way. The best thing that could have happened, besides the Reds winning, would have been me catching a ball. A ball did get hit into the stands, and it did come close to where we were sitting. But it took one bounce off the stadium steps and landed right in Samantha's lap. Samantha was sitting three seats away from me, just kind of staring blankly off into space. I'm not sure she even knew what a foul ball was. Actually, I'm not even sure she knew which teams were playing. She was probably sitting there thinking about some new rattle or something she was going to get for one of her Cabbage-Faces. Anyway, the ball landing on her lap like that startled her, and she jumped up. Before Grandad or Gram or I could grab it, the ball rolled off her lap. It rolled down to the next row of seats and the people sitting in front of us scrambled to claim it.

But those were minor drawbacks; the rest of the time was the greatest evening I'd ever had, even though I felt sort of sick in the car on the way home from all of the junk I had eaten.

Gram and Samantha both fell asleep on the backseat on the long drive back to the farm. That gave Grandad and me a chance to talk some more.

"Oliver," said Grandad. "If things were different, and you *had* found those missing baseball cards at our house, what would you have done with them? Would you have sold them and gotten a lot of money for them, or would you have traded them? Or do you think you would have kept them?"

I had to think about that for a minute. In my fantasies about finding the cards, I had never really gone past the point of actually finding them. Well, that's not completely true. I must admit that a few times I imagined that I had suddenly become famous for finding a spectacular lost card collection, just like that kid who found the Honus Wagner card. I imagined that because of my fame I was invited onto a television talk show, like the "Tonight Show." I pictured myself being interviewed by Jay Leno.

"Now, Oliver," Jay would say. "How did you feel when you opened the rusty old tin box and took out the Willie Mays rookie card, in perfect condition?"

"Well, Mr. Leno," I would answer, "I wish every kid in America could experience the excitement I felt when I first saw that card. When I first tasted the thrill of finding what I had been searching for. I guess it was just a matter of recognizing the clues and figuring it all out."

Yeah, that would have been terrific, all right.

But as to what I would have actually done with the cards after all the excitement and thrill of finding them had died down, I wasn't sure.

"Dad told me that I could keep them, if I found them," I said to Grandad. "And I'm sure they'd be worth a lot of money by now. He says he had some really outstanding cards."

"Well, then. Would you have sold them?" asked Grandad.

I had always liked the idea of coming into a large

amount of money. Visions of the riches that could be mine with the fortune I'd have made from selling my baseball cards came to mind: Nintendo games, a TV set for my room, a compact disk player—the list was endless, really. But if I sold the cards, I reasoned, then I wouldn't have them anymore. And it was the cards I wanted, really. I wanted to be able to take out that Willie Mays and look at it anytime I felt like it. I wanted to be able to have a Don Drysdale or a Stan Musial that I could point to and say, "That's *my* rare and valuable card. My father got that in a bubble gum pack years ago and saved it."

Only he hadn't saved it. That was the problem.

"You've learned a valuable lesson from this whole thing, Oliver," said Grandad.

Boy, grown-ups really love it when you learn a valuable lesson from something. No matter how much pain and suffering you had to go through, at least you were learning that valuable lesson.

"What possible lesson can I have learned?" I asked. Maybe how to live my life with major disappointment, I thought. I expected Grandad to come up with something like "that there's no use crying over spilt milk," or, "nothing ventured, nothing gained," or something like that.

Instead, he said, "Now you know that you should take very good care of your own baseball cards, the cards you're collecting now, as a boy. You should keep them in a safe place and in good condition. Someday you'll be able to give them to your own son, when you have one. Think how much *your* son will be able to appreciate the cards you're saving now."

That thought had never occurred to me. That *would* be pretty cool, having a son and giving him my baseball cards. That thought cheered me up a little. At least I could do that, even if I couldn't have my dad's cards. Only time would tell which of my cards would become valuable. I had a suspicion, though, that some of the guys whose cards I was saving now were going to turn out to be some of the greats in baseball history. After all, as I told you before, I study statistics carefully and chart the progress of the players. I collect baseball cards very scientifically. I'm pretty sure that when I grow up, my collection will be really spectacular, maybe even better than the one Dad had.

Of course, all that will be a long time in the future, but at least it's something to think about.

♦

The rest of the time we were at Gram and Grandad's, I managed to enjoy myself just doing some fun things around the farm. Grandad and I went back to the little clubhouse in the woods and fixed it up. Grandad tore down the rest of the vines that covered it, so that light could come in through the windows. I swept out the twigs and leaves and cleaned it up inside. I thought about saving those Oreo cookies for science class, but the more I looked at them, the more I wasn't sure what they actually were. And since I didn't know what they were, I didn't really want to have them hanging around.

The clubhouse looked great when we were finished. My friend Tad, from the stable, came over, and we played alien invaders and military command station. Grandad brought up an old bike of Dad's from the basement and fixed it up for me. He repaired the tires and bought a new seat. I attached Samantha's Reds pennant to the handlebars (she said I could have it; once she got it home she really couldn't find any use for it, herself). The effect was pretty classy, if I do say so myself, especially since the bike was red. Tad and I took some long rides along the country roads around the farm.

I even joined Gram and Samantha in their baking frenzy. I helped them make brownies one day—I mixed the batter, and when the brownies were finished, put a pecan in the center of each square. Another day, they made pizza from scratch. I helped out with that, too, kneading the dough and doing an awesome job. The most fun of it, though, was when I started flicking little dough balls at Samantha. She kept looking at the ceiling because she couldn't figure out what was happening and thought things were falling on her. The next thing you knew, we were having a full-fledged dough fight, and Gram was chasing us out of the kitchen, waving the flyswatter at us.

Before long, it was the day before Mom and Dad were supposed to come and pick us up. The time had gone by so fast; I would have liked to stay another week or so. But I did have some friends back home who had gotten a three-week head start on summer vacation without me. I wondered what they had been up to. I looked forward to playing some baseball and tennis, and to just hanging out with the guys, although hanging out with Tad had been fun, too. I did kind of miss Mom and Dad, and of course, I missed my baseball card collection.

"Oliver," said Gram that evening. "Do you remember that you promised to try on some of these old clothes of your father's before you leave for home?"

Oh-oh. I had almost forgotten. Better yet, Gram had almost forgotten. But not quite. The last thing I felt like doing was trying on old clothes of my dad's. Even if they did fit, I was going to try to get out of actually wearing them once I got them home. No way was I going to go out in public in geek clothes.

"Come on, Oliver," said Grandad. "Throw in the towel, and do it for Gram. After all, you can kill two birds with one stone. You can make your grandmother happy, and you might get some new duds out of the deal."

New duds that could possibly make me the laughingstock of Millard Fillmore Elementary, I thought. One day of wearing a madras shirt could destroy my reputation for years to come.

"Oh, all right." I sighed. Maybe I could take them home with me without Mom seeing them and stuff them in the back of my closet, never to be heard from again. Or maybe they would have a sixties day at school, and I would have a good excuse for wearing a pink-and-orange-flowered shirt and a green mohair sweater. And there was always Halloween.

Gram handed me a pair of jeans to try on. Those looked pretty decent, until I got them on and looked at myself in the full-length mirror.

"Oh, no!" I said. "Bell-bottoms! I've got to draw the line at that! I can't wear bell-bottoms!"

Gram sighed in defeat. "Oh, all right, Oliver, we wouldn't want you to go around looking like you're not the last word in coolness. Okay, I'll take these clothes down to the homeless shelter in town. Maybe some young boy who cares more about being warm than cool will be happy to have them."

That made me feel a little guilty, but not so guilty that I wanted to wear bell-bottoms.

Then Gram held up a heavy winter jacket. It was bright red with a picture of a horse's head on the back and a swirling rope design across the shoulders and down the sleeves. That actually looked kind of interesting. You had to wonder, if you wore a jacket like that, would it be so different that it would actually be cool? It was a fine line. At least you'd be a standout in any crowd. It would be a swell jacket to wear if you were working on a road crew and had to direct traffic. No one could possibly miss seeing you.

"Hey, there's something in this pocket," I said, my right hand closing over a small object. I pulled out the small object; it was a pocketknife, probably left there years ago by my dad.

"This is neat," I said, opening it up. There were three different blades, a nail file, a can opener, and some other little gadget that I couldn't quite figure out.

I stuck my hand down in the other pocket and felt around. Maybe there would be something else. And there was. This time my hand closed over another object, a small, rectangular shape. I brought my hand out of my pocket and stared in utter disbelief at the object I held.

It was a pack of cards, held tightly together with a rubber band. On the top card, looking back at me, was the smiling face of Sandy Koufax.

Still wearing the horse jacket, I sank to the living room floor. I took the rubber band off and started laying out the cards on the floor, faceup: Whitey Ford; Stan Musial; Ernie Banks at home plate; Juan Marichal, winding up to pitch; Warren Spahn; Ted Williams, making contact with the ball; Bob Gibson.

I couldn't believe my eyes.

Gram and Grandad and Samantha were gathered around me now, excitedly watching and making comments, but I was in a daze, completely unaware of what they were saying. Finally, Gram broke through my fog, and I heard her say, "Oliver. Oliver, listen. Look in the inside pockets."

"What, Gram?" I looked up at her.

"The inside pockets. There should be two inside pockets in that coat."

I reached inside the jacket on the left side and found the pocket. I groped around in the pocket and pulled out another packet of baseball cards, with Roberto Clemente's picture on the top card. Then I reached into the inside pocket on the right side. Still another pack, tightly bound with a rubber band. Was I dreaming, or what? I had found the treasure. I had found it, and I had found it totally by accident.

I started laughing, I was so overjoyed. Gram and Grandad started laughing with me. Samantha couldn't figure out why we were laughing, but she didn't want to feel left out, so she started laughing, too.

"Ollie boy," said Grandad. "You worked long and hard to find those cards, and I have to say . . ."

He paused for a moment and I knew he was searching his mind for the perfect saying for this situation.

"Well," he said finally. "I guess it all only goes to show—there's more than one way to skin a cat!"

♦

So now I have *the* most serious baseball card collection that I've ever heard about, or that anyone I know has ever heard about. Now when grown-ups say to me, "Boy, if I only had the baseball cards I collected when I was a kid—" I say proudly, "Guess what? My dad *did* save his cards. And *I* found them!"

I admit that sometimes, as I'm going over my collection, carefully handling my vintage Ted Williams, or reading the stats on the back of my 1957 Brooks Robinson, I think about how much all these cards are worth. I think about what I could do with the money I'd get from selling just a few of my valuable collector cards.

But then I remember how much I'd miss having them to touch and look at. And I remember how much fun it's going to be when I'm an old guy like Dad. I'll be able to show these cards to my son and tell him stories about how great those players were. I'll tell him about how I collected baseball cards, and how I visited the Hall of Fame and saw the Babe's original bat. I'll tell him about how I went to a night game at Riverfront Stadium to see the Reds play, and how a ball fell into my sister's lap. And then, of course, I'll tell him all about a fantastic summer, long ago, when I searched for and finally found my father's long-lost baseball card collection.

EDISON TWP. FREE PUBLIC LIBRARY